LAURENT DE BRUNHOFF

BABAR'S
Book of Color

ABRAMS BOOKS FOR YOUNG READERS, NEW YORK

One morning when Babar was in his studio, his children Flora, Pom and Alexander came to see him, bringing Cousin Arthur.

"Can we use some of your paints, Papa?" Pom asked. "We want to paint, too."

"Of course," said Babar. "Why don't each of you pick a color—red, blue, yellow, white, or black—and paint what it makes you think of."

RED

"I want red," Flora said and painted two red cherries to hang on her ears.

"I want red, too," said Alexander, "so I can paint a lobster."

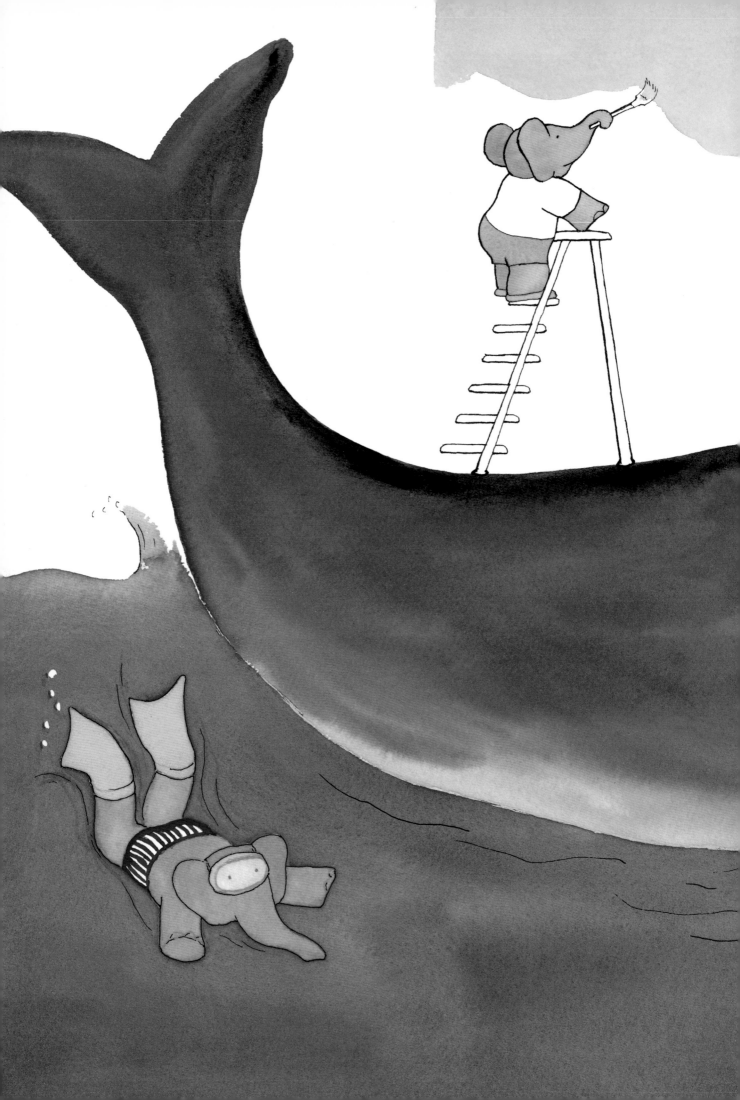

BLUE

"My favorite color is blue," said Pom, and he painted a pale blue sky over a big blue whale in the great blue ocean.

YELLOW

"I'm going to paint myself a whole swarm of yellow jackets," said Alexander.

WHITE

"What will you paint with white? Don't forget white," said Babar.

"Snow!" said Alexander.

"A polar bear," said Pom.

"A snow elephant," said Flora.

WHITE

"And what will you paint with black?" asked Babar.
"A black cat," said Arthur.
"Blackbirds," said Alexander.

BLACK

"Excellent work!" said Babar. "Now I will show you how to make more colors from just the ones you have." He blew up three balloons—one red, one yellow, one blue.

"Look!" he said, pulling two balloons together. "If you mix two colors you get a third. If you mix all three you get black. Let me see what you can do when you mix colors together."

GREEN

Pom mixed yellow with his favorite, blue, and made green, which he and Flora used to paint frogs and crocodiles.

ORANGE

Flora gave Alexander some red to mix with
his yellow. This gave them a bright
orange for painting pumpkins.

PURPLE

Last they mixed red and blue to get purple, a beautiful color for a car for Queen Celeste.

GRAY

Babar suggested that Flora add a little black to some white. She was delighted to find she had gray.

"Now I can paint a big herd of elephants," she said.

PINK

"And now try adding a little red to the white, Flora," said Babar.

"Pink," she said. "Lovely, lovely pink! I've always wanted pink flamingos on my walls."

BROWN

"Brown is the hardest color to make," said Babar, "but I will help you. Mix red, blue, and yellow with just a little bit of black, and paint me a bear."

"I'll give you one more color," said Babar, "but then we have to get ready for dinner. Mix the brown you made with a little yellow and a dash of white and you will have tan and can paint yourselves camels."

What a pleasant afternoon they had playing with color. Babar hung the artwork on a display board in his studio, making the children very proud.

The Library of Congress has cataloged the original Abrams edition of this book as follows:

Brunhoff, Laurent de, 1925-
Babar's Book of Color / Laurent de Brunhoff.
p. cm.
Summary: Pom, Flora, Alexander, and Arthur go to Babar' studio
and learn about mixing and using colors.
ISBN 978-0-8109-4840-2
[1. Color—Fiction. 2. Elephants—Fiction.] I. Title.

PZ7.B82843Babj 2004
[E]—dc22

2003013235

ISBN for this edition: 978-1-4197-0339-3

Printed and bound in China

10 9 8 7 6 5 4 3 2 1

Abrams Books for Young Readers are available at special discounts
when purchased in quantity for premiums and promotions as well as fundraising or educational use.
Special editions can also be created to specification. For details,
contact specialsales@abramsbooks.com or the address below.

THE ART OF BOOKS SINCE 1949
115 West 18th Street
New York, NY 10011
www.abramsbooks.com